Introduction

As a society, we abhor the idea of children being sexual. Wanting our children *innocent*, we provide them with extremely negative messages about sexuality, and we push them away from appropriate and positive information. Being *emotionally barefoot* regarding sexuality, we teach critical or silly words about genitalia, and we make children fearful of normal sexual curiosity. Through our *Purple Faces*, we teach children that we are uncomfortable and irritated with their sexual questions. From a very early age, children learn shame and embarrassment about sexual issues.

As we are troubled by the thought that our children might be sexual, we become absolutely devastated by the thought that our children might be sexually abused. We feel so angry and upset about sexual molestation that our prevention efforts tend to reflect our hostility. We use words such as *bad* to describe sexual contact, making children feel badly about the entire subject. When abusers are presented as evil, and when they face harsh consequences for their crime, children become frightened and suspicious. We rarely give children any positive information that might create a sense of self-protection. Children learn fear and apprehension from typical prevention efforts, rather than safety and security.

In spite of our best intentions, our negative approach to child sexuality and sexual abuse prevention actually helps sex offenders abuse our precious children. Child abusers are aware of the embarrassment and discomfort that exists between children and adults regarding sexual issues. They actively use this negative atmosphere to their advantage. Recognizing that children feel shameful and uncomfortable about sexuality, sex offenders correctly conclude that communication with adults will be resisted and avoided by children. Sexual privacy with the child is assured. Most abusers establish a relationship with children, making it easy to manipulate, bribe and coerce them into feeling like partners, rather than sexual victims. The child feels as if he/she has done something wrong and forbidden. The child feels guilty. The offender has enveloped the child in the sexual conspiracy, and the child must retreat to secrecy. In spite of our revulsion to sexual abuse, in spite of how much we care about our children, we have inadvertently made our children more vulnerable and easier to sexually abuse.

A positive approach to sexual abuse prevention is the solution to this dilemma. We cannot begin to prevent or detect sexual abuse without first opening positive communication with children about sexual issues. *A Very Touching Book* establishes a warm and positive foundation for sexuality before the issues of detection and prevention are addressed. Whether in a home, school, police station, social agency, church or treatment center, adults who read this book to a child, will teach positive ideas about sexuality, and they will begin the communication process.

Through the use of humor, *A Very Touching Book* encourages children and adults to hold, cuddle, laugh, care, share and most importantly, TALK. Like no other approach, giggles and laughter pervade this book—not for the purpose of discounting or minimizing the subject, but to bring children and adults together with warmth and tenderness. Through humor, fear and embarrassment fade, and communication begins.

Rather than using a negative or fearful term, *A Very Touching Book* refers to sexual abuse as *secret touching*. This term is explained in a way that creates a positive attitude toward adult sexuality, encouraging the privacy and uniqueness of our bodies <u>as children</u>. Children from toddlers to teenagers, learn to take pride in avoiding sexual contact while they are children because adult sexuality is viewed as something *special*—something to be valued. Like no other prevention approach *A Very Touching Book* gives children a reason to protect themselves.

The concept of secret touching also sets up a framework that allows children to judge whether contact with adults is appropriate or inappropriate, depending on the issues of *secrets*. Rather than teaching children to be fearful of any physical contact with adults, *A Very Touching Book* teaches children how to assess each situation according to the secrecy involved. This avoids giving a negative connotation to sexuality, to genitalia, or to the child. Affection and tenderness with adults can be encouraged, because children are given a way to protect themselves.

Most importantly, the idea of *secret touching* provides a natural solution to the problem by encouraging children to TELL about an unwanted sexual contact. By using this unique approach to the *secret problem*, we have encouraged our children to turn to us so that we can help them.

Through fear and embarrassment, children turn away from us to be abused and damaged. Through positive communication, sexual abuse can be detected and prevented.

This book is for big people who care about little people.

A special thanks
to the TOUCHING TEAM
in Malheur County, Oregon*

*District Attorney's Office
Juvenile Department
Mental Health Center
Children's Services
Law Enforcement

First Edition Copyright © 1983 by Jan Hindman
Reprinted 1984
New Edition (Revised) Copyright © 1985 by Jan Hindman
Reprinted 1990
Reprinted 1991
Reprinted 1992

Published by:
AlexAndria Associates
911 SW 3rd St.
Ontario, Oregon 97914
(503) 889-8938

I.S.B.N. 0-9611034-1-8

Printed in the United States of America

Northwest Printing, Inc., Boise, Idaho 83707

A VERY TOUCHING BOOK

...for little people and for big people...

by Jan Hindman

illustrated by Tom Novak / designed by Bob Foree

This is a book about a very special thing called

TOUCHING

This is the TOUCHING TEAM

and they are a special group of little folks who sort of look like fairies. They know lots and lots about kids and even more about this thing called TOUCHING.

Let's start with what the word TOUCH means.

tutch'ing v. when two or more things come together. When one thing is right next to, or joining with another thing, then a touch happens.

Touch right here to turn the page

We touch things everyday and every minute.

If you blow and blow and blow a big, big, big bubble with your bubble gum.. your gum may touch your nose and make a big mess.

If you eat a juicy, smooshy, gooshy piece of watermelon... your mouth may touch the watermelon and also make a big mess. (It will look like you have watermelon lips.)

Right now, you are touching some things even while you read this book. Can you name some?

Of course, we all know that things are different from people. People are different from socks and sand and Silly Putty. The biggest difference is that people can feel, and things can't feel.

It is feeling that makes touching things different from touching people. People-touching and feelings go together.

There are lots of different feelings. Take a look at this: let's say you have a nice friend who always gives you 3 bites of her mustard and jelly sandwich. You feel nice about this friend, and when you touch her... it feels nice too.

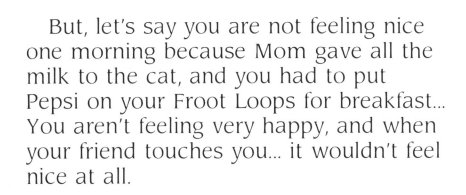

But, let's say you are not feeling nice one morning because Mom gave all the milk to the cat, and you had to put Pepsi on your Froot Loops for breakfast... You aren't feeling very happy, and when your friend touches you... it wouldn't feel nice at all.

There are lots and lots of different
kinds of feelings such as:

happy   sad   scared   angry

The different kinds of feelings help us understand the different kinds of touching. So, now that you know all about different kinds of feelings, let's pack up those feelings and take a look at **people-touching.**

Here we go!
There are 3 kinds of touching. The first kind makes us feel good. We will call it

good touching.

There are many ways that people can touch each other and feel good.

Maybe while you are reading this, you should touch another person by holding their hand or sitting on their lap, just so we know how good people-touching can be.

Give them a big smile too... just to get the good feeling started.

The second kind of touching makes
us feel very different than good
touching. This kind of touching makes
us feel bad.
We will call it

bad touching. Bad touching hurts!

There are many ways that people can
touch each other and feel bad because
of the hurts.

The third kind of touching is the hardest to understand because we have so many different kinds of feelings about it... both good and bad.

Remember back a few pages when we talked about all the different kinds of feelings? Well, this third kind of touching gives us many, many, many, feelings.

This kind of touching is about special parts of our bodies. Let's stop and talk about those special parts for a minute or two...

For a girl, two very special parts of her body are on her chest and between her legs. These are terrific parts, so pay close attention to this.

On her chest are two bumps. Actually, her chest looks the same as the chest of a boy.

We know, however, that when she grows older, these bumps will grow into two wonderful things called breasts.

Breasts are great things to have when you are older.

The other special part of a girl's body is between her legs. She has a small opening to something called a vagina.

The vagina is on the inside so you really can't see it. What you can see are two special parts that look like lips. These special lips are called the vulva and they take very good care of the vagina on the inside.

Vaginas and vulvas are great when you are older too.

Sometimes, we use silly names for those special parts of our bodies.

People get

purple faces

when they talk about those parts. That is usually because they don't know the right word, and they use a silly word to cover up their purple faces.

You could have a giggle gaggle right now if you want to, just to get rid of the purple faces. Have a grown-up help you, and, together, think of all the silly words we have for a girl's special parts. Say each word out loud and giggle and giggle and giggle about each word.

Then, after all that giggling, throw those silly words away, because now you know the right words for those wonderful parts of a girl's body.

Make sure the grown-up reading this with you knows how to say the right words. Grown-ups are usually the ones with purple faces so they need the most help in learning the right words.

Help the grown-up say each word... 3 times... with a smile... v e r y s l o w l y.

vagina   breasts   vulva
vagina   breasts   vulva
vagina   breasts   vulva

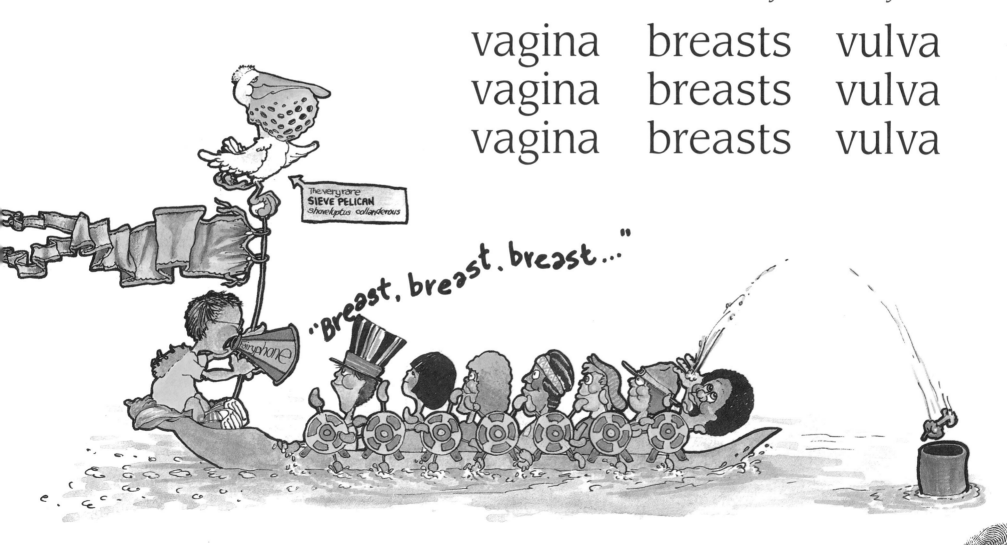

Check for purple faces.

Tell the grown-up, "Good Job!"

Now, let's talk about boys.

Boys have special parts, too, and those special parts are between their legs just like with little girls. These are wonderful parts and boys should be very happy with them.

A boy has a penis and two very special things called testicles.

The penis is the longer pointed part, and the testicles are rounder and smaller and hang just below the penis.

Boys are very proud of their penises and testicles when they get older, just like girls are proud of their special parts.

Again, you should remember that some people, especially grown-ups, use silly names for these wonderful parts. They get purple faces because they don't know the right words to use.

You may need to have another giggle gaggle just to get rid of the purple faces.

Make sure the grown-up reading this with you can say the right words...
3 times... with a smile... v e r y s l o w l y.

penis   testicles
penis   testicles
penis   testicles

Watch for purple faces!

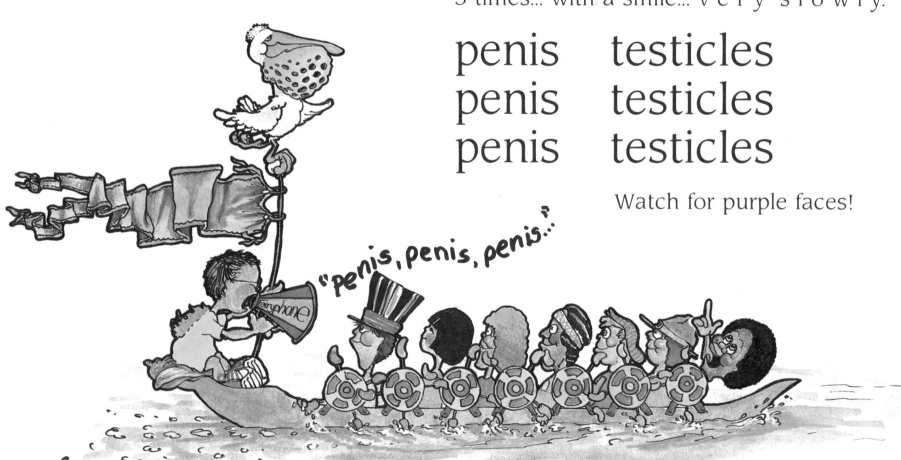

Now that
we know all
about the right words
for all of those wonderful,
special parts for boys and girls,
we need to know why all the fuss
about those parts.

The reason those parts are so special is
that something terrific happens to them.
When you are older and more grown-up,
you can share those parts of your body with
someone very... very... very... special.

Grown-ups share those parts of their bodies
with another special grown-up, and it's
a wonderful thing...
for grown-ups that is.

There are 2 very big reasons
why the sharing of those
parts is such a
great thing.

First, while we are growing up, we keep those parts of our bodies very special and private. When we keep things special and private, that means we don't share them with our friends, our neighbors or... for instance, the people at the supermarket.

If you stop and think about it, we don't share those special parts of our bodies like we do, say, our elbows and ears.

Wouldn't it be silly if it were backwards and we kept our elbows and ears special and private but shared our special parts with everyone?

That really would be silly, wouldn't it?

We usually wear clothes to keep those parts covered, private and special. Even on the hottest day of the year, when we need to take off lots of our clothes just to keep cool... we still keep those special parts private.

Remember, we don't cover those parts because they are silly or ugly or nasty. We cover them and keep them private because they are special and like no other part of our body.

By keeping those parts private and not sharing them...

with your friends on the school bus...

with Santa at the shopping mall...

with mom's friends at the beauty shop...

with people at the restaurant...

... we are able to keep those parts special. That's what makes sharing them with someone when you grow up a great thing.

Another way to understand this idea of keeping things special and private would be to think about this silly idea.

Suppose we have Christmas tomorrow... and you get to have a big dinner, open presents and have lots of company. But then the next day it is Christmas again... and then the next day, again... and again... and again... and on... and on... and on.

What would happen to the special idea of Christmas if we had it everyday? You see, if we don't keep those parts special, the sharing of those parts wouldn't be a big deal at all, just like Christmas wouldn't be a big deal if we had it every day.

The second reason that the sharing of those parts is such a big deal is that grown-ups need to spend a lot of time thinking about who the special person will be that they decide to share their bodies with.

This usually happens after they have thought... and thought... and thought... and thought.

They wait and think and wonder.

They look and talk and meet lots of people before they can pick the right person. The longer they think and the more they plan, the better the choice is and the more exciting and wonderful it is—once it happens.

This is a very hard decision. When we are kids, we don't have time to worry about that kind of decision. We are too busy deciding things like

do we want peppermint chip or blueberry nugget ice cream... do we want a black puppy or a brown puppy... or do we want to watch cartoons or creepy creatures on T.V.?

Choosing someone to share your body with is a big decision, and only grown-ups should decide about that. It is too big of a decision for kids,

even for SUPER KIDS LIKE YOU!

Now, let's get back to the idea of touching.

The third kind of touching is called

secret touching.

It happens when an older or bigger person touches a child's special parts and makes it a secret.

Remember, kids can't decide yet who to share their special parts with, and they are also working very hard to keep those parts special and private. That is why it is not okay for a grown-up or older person to be touching a child's special parts and making it a secret.

The grown-up or older person knows this kind of touching is not okay for kids, and they know that they are making a big mistake. They need to keep it a secret so no one will find out.

Now something needs to be said about secrets. Do you know what a secret is?

see'krit n. a secret is something that you can't tell anyone. It makes you feel funny. It is a strange, sometimes exciting, feeling. Sometimes secrets make your tummy feel like it is doing flip flops.

Some secrets are okay... and lots of fun, like the secret about your birthday presents...

like the secret about who is wearing the ghost costume...

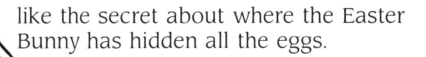

like the secret about where the Easter Bunny has hidden all the eggs.

Those secrets are fun and exciting, especially when everyone gets to find out, and the secret is over. But there should never be a secret about the touching of special parts between grown-ups and kids!

Sometimes grown-ups need to touch the special parts of children. This touching is okay if the child doesn't feel like they need to keep the touching a secret.

Let's see if you can tell when the touching of special parts is okay or not okay, depending on secrets.

Sometimes a doctor needs to touch you and your special parts to make sure you are not sick.

If Mom or Dad or the nurse is in the same room with you, and you can hurry home and tell your sister how brave you were when the doctor touched those special parts, is that a secret kind of touching?

TOUCH THE RIGHT ANSWER

Remember, secrets are when you can't tell, and no one else knows about it. So even if Mom and Dad weren't in the room, but you told them later about how brave you were, that would not be secret touching.

Let's try again.

Sometimes parents need to touch special parts to help their kids... like maybe when they change a baby's diaper.

Let's say Mom is in the kitchen cooking a big pot of spaghetti, and she begins to have trouble. Your baby sister decides to make a big surprise in her pants. (You know how that is.) Well, Dad has to change the baby's pants, and so, he will need to touch all over her special parts.

Now if you and Mom and the cat and everyone else is there... smiling at Dad's wrinkled up nose, is that a touching secret?

TOUCH THE RIGHT ANSWER

Let's try one more time. This will be the hardest riddle about secret touching.

Pretend that you visit Grandma and Grandpa in the country. While Grandpa is fishing, you decide to play in the mooshy, gooshy mud. When Grandpa says it's time to go to the house for dinner, you realize something funny has happened. You have, crawling around inside your pants, 6 frogs, 8 pollywogs, 2 grasshoppers, and 1 toothless turtle. Since Grandpa smells a little *fishy*, you both decide to jump in the shower and start scrubbing. You need to get real clean before Grandma comes back from the garden.

Since you are soooooooo dirty, you are going to need some help getting clean. Your special parts will have to be scrubbed too, so Grandpa is going to help.

Now... you are alone with Grandpa... your special parts are going to be touched. Is that a touching secret???

Would it be a secret if as soon as Grandma gets back, you tell her that you were so dirty you needed help with your shower—even scrubbing your special parts—and that you will give her lots of help cleaning the critters out of the bathroom???

TOUCH THE RIGHT ANSWER

The answer you should have touched is

NO!

These are not touching secrets because you can always tell someone, or someone knows about the touching.

Secret touching happens when an older or bigger person touches your special parts and makes you feel that you can't tell.

Secret touching may happen in the dark or in another secret place, and you may feel so, so alone... and too afraid to tell.

Secret touching may happen with someone you love a lot! Someone whom you would feel bad about getting into trouble if you told the touching secret.

Secret touching may happen with a trick... or a promise not to tell about the touching. You may be promised treats or fun or extra love. You may not feel like telling because you want the special things.

Secret touching may happen with a
person so... so... so... big and important
that you feel too... too... too... little to tell.

Although kids are smaller, the important thing to remember is that kids are people too. This means that kids have rights, especially about touching.

We all know that kids need help from grown-ups, and bigger people. We need to respect grown-ups and usually we need to do as they tell us to do. But, when it comes to touching, both grown-ups and kids need to understand that kids have special rights!

SECRET TOUCHING IS NOT OKAY FOR KIDS because kids have a right to keep those very wonderful parts of their bodies special and private, so that when they grow up and want to share those parts with someone special, it will be a terrific thing.

SECRET TOUCHING IS NOT OKAY FOR KIDS because kids have a right to choose someone to share their body with when they grow up. If a grown-up or bigger person touches a kid's special parts, then it cheats the kid out of getting to make their own choice later... when they are older and know a whole lot more about such things.

SECRET TOUCHING IS NOT OKAY FOR KIDS because kids have a right to feel happy and proud of their special parts. If secret touching happens to kids, they may miss out on feeling great about those parts... and that's not fair... since it is the grown-up who is making the mistake.

Big people and little people should remember that:

The most important right of all is a kid's right to say.....

to any kind of secret touching

even though you may be offered treats,
even though you are little,
even though you may care about the person,
even though you may be scared,
even though touching those parts may feel good

YOU CAN SAY NO

Now, put on your thinking caps.

What should a kid do about good touching ?

Get lots & lots & lots
& lots & lots
& lots

What should a kid do about bad touching ?

Try not to give it, try not to get it.

What should a kid do about secret touching **?**

Even if you are confused and not sure if it's secret touching, TELL SOMEONE so they can help you decide.

If you tell someone about secret touching or about any touching you don't understand, then it won't be a secret anymore.

If you tell someone, the secret will stop, and everyone will feel better.

Secrets about touching are too heavy for kids. Kids need to be kids and not have to worry about the kind of touching that is only for grown-ups.

There are lots of people who can help you with the secrets:

a teacher,
a policeman,
a Mom or Dad,
a sister or brother,
a school counselor...

... and probably the person or grown-up who was nice enough to read this book with you. They would be an especially good person to tell since they know all about touching and kids and kid's rights.

Now that you know all about touching...
goodbye... good luck...
and

good

touching!